Copyright © 2002 by Michael Neugebauer Verlag, an imprint of
Nord-Süd Verlag AG, Gossau Zürich, Switzerland
First published in Switzerland under the title *Ich will nicht allein schlafen.*
English translation © 2002 by North-South Books Inc., New York

First published in the United States, Great Britain, Canada,
Australia, and New Zealand in 2002 by North-South Books,
an imprint of Nord-Süd Verlag AG, Gossau Zürich, Switzerland.

Distributed in the United States by North-South Books Inc., New York.

Library of Congress Cataloging-in-Publication Data is available.
A CIP catalogue record for this book is available from The British Library.
ISBN 0-7358-1602-6 (trade edition) 10 9 8 7 6 5 4 3 2 1
ISBN 0-7358-1603-4 (library edition) 10 9 8 7 6 5 4 3 2 1
Printed in Germany

For more information about our books, and the authors and artists
who create them, visit our web site: www.northsouth.com

It's Bedtime!

By Brigitte Weninger

Illustrated by Alan Marks

Translated by Kathryn Grell

A MICHAEL NEUGEBAUER BOOK

North-South Books

New York • London

"It's bedtime!" called Mother.
"Say good night to everyone."

"Good night, Daddy," said Ben.
"Good night, Grandmother.
 Good night, Kitty.
 Good night, television!"

"Come along, Ben," said Mother.
"I'll tuck you in now."

"I don't want to sleep alone," Ben whined.

"You're not alone," said Mother. "You have all your stuffed toys to keep you company."

"Do you want Teddy to sleep next to you tonight?"
asked Mother. "He can hold your water bottle and
give you a drink if you get thirsty."

"No. I don't want Teddy!" said Ben.

"What about Minnie?" asked Mother. "She's very cuddly."

"No, I don't want Minnie either," Ben replied.

"What about Bingo?" asked Mother. "He can even bring you your slippers in the morning."

"No, not Bingo," said Ben.

"Maybe you'd like to have your clown tonight," suggested Mother. "He's lots of fun."

"No, I don't want the clown!" Ben insisted.

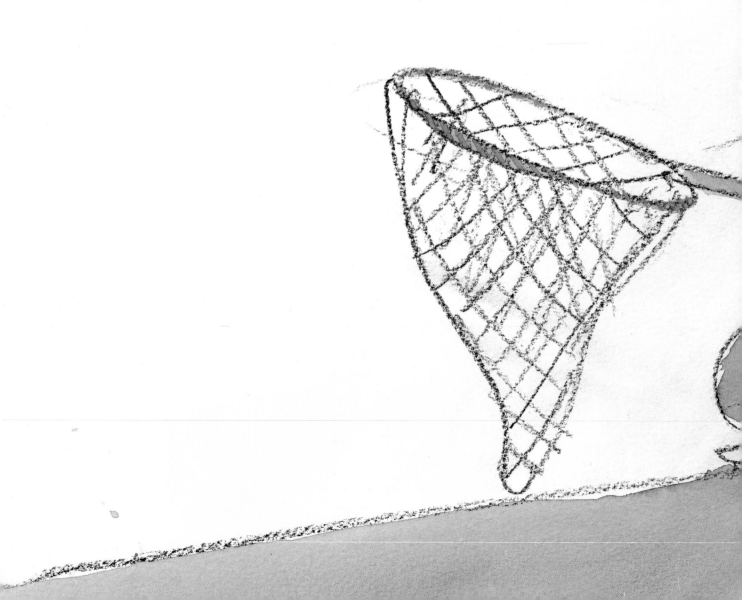

"Well, that just leaves your
Davy doll," said Mother.

"But I don't *want* Davy!"
said Ben.

"Well then," said Mother, "who *do* you want?"

"Him!" declared Ben.

"Oh, no! Not *him*," said Mother.

"Oh, YES!" Ben said firmly.

"But he is *terrible*!"
said Mother.

"I know," said Ben. "He is very terrible—and strong and mean. And that's why I want him. He will scare away the ghosts and monsters and keep me safe."

Then Ben snuggled down happily and went to sleep.